R9-00

SUSAN LACY

Mussarat's Monster

Illustrated by Amanda Welch

Methuen Children's Books

First published in Great Britain 1988
by Methuen Children's Books Ltd
11 New Fetter Lane, London EC4P 4EE
Text copyright © 1988 Susan Lacy
Illustrations copyright © 1988 Amanda Welch
Printed in Great Britain
by St Edmundsbury Press, Bury St Edmunds, Suffolk

British Library Cataloguing in Publication Data

Lacy, Susan
  Mussarat's Monster – (A Read aloud book).
  I. Title   II. Welch, Amanda   III. Series
  823'.914[J]   PZ7

  ISBN 0-416-04322-4

Contents

1
The Bubble Gum Monster

One afternoon on the way home from school Mussarat and her little brother Asif stopped outside the sweet shop. They both had a 10p piece to spend, but what were they going to buy?

"I'm putting my money in the bubble gum machine," said Asif at last.

He put his money in the slot and out rolled a little red plastic ball. He opened it, and inside was a silver ring and a soft, fat, chewy ball of bubble gum.

Mussarat put her money in the bubble gum machine too. She turned the handle and out rolled a little yellow ball, just like Asif's.

"I wonder what's inside it," she said. "I hope I get a silver ring like yours."

She twisted it and turned it. She pulled it and pushed it. But the little yellow ball stayed shut.

1

"It must be stuck," Mussarat decided, putting it into her coat pocket. "I'll try to open it again when we get home."

Mum was in the kitchen making chapattis for tea.

"Hurry up, you two, you're late," she shouted as Mussarat and Asif came through the door. "Go and take your coats off, and don't forget to wash your hands."

Mussarat hung her coat up and took the yellow ball out of her pocket. She ran upstairs to her bedroom and stood it carefully on top of the tall cupboard near the wall.

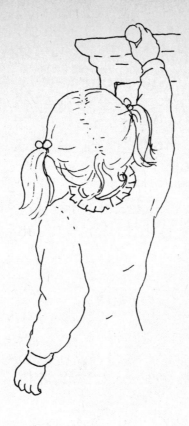

Downstairs her big sister Shazia was busy giving the baby his tea. And Asif was busy eating round, fat, buttery chapattis. Mussarat sat down quickly before he ate them all.

"Greedy thing," she said. "Leave some chapattis for me." And she forgot all about the little yellow ball.

It was the middle of the night. Mussarat woke up with a jump. She opened her eyes wide and looked around. What had woken her? It couldn't be her big sister Shazia, because she was fast asleep in the bed near the wall. It couldn't be Asif or the baby, because they were fast asleep in the bedroom next door.

Mussarat sat up and listened. What was that noise? Was it Shazia, talking in her

sleep? Or the tree outside the window, creaking in the wind? Or . . . she stared at the cupboard near the wall. The little yellow ball on top of it was glowing in the dark. Then, as she watched, it started to dance. It hopped and jumped, twisted and turned, skipped and skated, until, quivering and quaking, it rolled to the edge and fell to the floor with a bump.

Mussarat shut her eyes and pulled the covers over her head. Perhaps if she kept very quiet whatever it was would go away.

After what seemed like hours, she opened her eyes and pulled the covers slowly right down to her nose. The little yellow ball was sitting on the carpet. It was quiet now and didn't move at all, even when she tiptoed towards it.

Mussarat knelt down. She put out her hand and touched the yellow ball with a finger. It was warm and soft – and suddenly, it sneezed! Mussarat fell back against the bed in surprise as a little yellow nose appeared. The little yellow ball sneezed again. Then it shivered and stretched until two little arms and two little legs grew out of its fat little body. Two green eyes opened wide

and stared at Mussarat. Mussarat stared
back. Then the little creature closed its eyes,
curled into a ball and went to sleep.

When Mussarat woke again the sun was
shining through the bedroom window. She
rubbed her eyes. Had she been dreaming?
Did the yellow ball really come alive last
night? She threw back her covers and
climbed out of bed. No, she hadn't been
dreaming. There, on the carpet, sat the little
yellow creature. It blinked at Mussarat and
Mussarat blinked back. She touched it
gently. The creature was warm and soft and
made a purring sound as she stroked it.

Shazia turned over in bed.

"Is it time to get up yet, Mussarat?" she asked, and yawned loudly.

The little animal curled tightly into a ball. Mussarat picked it up.

"Don't make so much noise, you've frightened it," she told Shazia.

"Frightened what?" Shazia sat up and stared at the tiny yellow creature. "What is it?" she whispered. "Where did you find it?"

Mussarat smiled. "I don't know what it is. I bought it from the sweet shop yesterday."

Shazia shivered. "Well, I think you ought to take it back. Come downstairs and show it to Mum and Dad."

Mum was in the kitchen making tea. Dad was eating his breakfast and the baby was sitting on Asif's knee.

"What do you want for breakfast, girls?" asked Mum, looking up. "Ugh!" she screamed, and dropped a cup with a loud crash on to the floor.

Dad glanced round quickly.

"What's the matter," he said. "Come and eat your . . ." He stared at Mussarat. "What on earth have you got in your hand?"

Mussarat put the creature down on the table.

"I don't know," she said softly, "but I'd like to keep it, Dad."

The little yellow ball opened its green eyes wide and looked at Dad. It shuffled towards

him and sneezed loudly. Suddenly Dad laughed. Then Mum laughed, and Shazia laughed, and even Asif and the baby laughed.

"I think it likes you, Dad," said Mussarat.

Mussarat and Asif ran all the way home from school that afternoon.

"Is it all right, Mum?" Mussarat asked as she pushed open the kitchen door.

Mum was sitting at the table with the baby on her knees.

"I don't know," she said, and pointed to the floor. The little creature was fast asleep in a cardboard box, curled up on Asif's old woolly jumper. "It hasn't eaten anything all day. I've tried bread and milk and chapattis. And the baby tried hard with his dinner. But it's no good." She shook her head sadly and the baby shook his.

"But it's got to eat something," Mussarat whispered as she knelt beside it.

"It must be hungry," said Asif, "and I'm hungry too. Can I have a banana, please?" Asif took a banana from the fruit bowl. He sat down next to the box and began to peel it.

The little yellow creature uncurled slowly. It opened its green eyes wide. It stared at

Mussarat, then at Asif, and sneezed loudly.
Then it sneezed again. And again and again.

"I think it's trying to tell us something,"
said Asif.

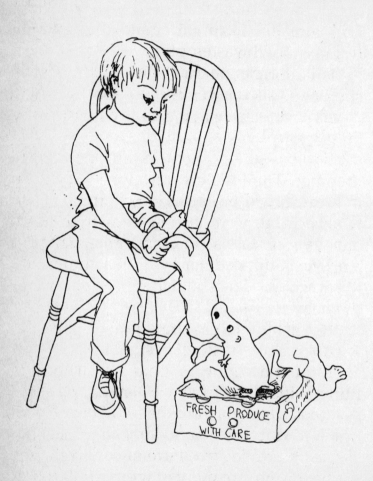

Mussarat smiled. "I think it's trying to tell you something. I think it wants your banana."

And sure enough, when Asif held it out, the little creature swallowed it in one gulp, skin and all. Then another and another until the fruit bowl was empty.

Every morning before she went to school, Mussarat called at the fruit shop. And every day the little yellow creature grew bigger and bigger. Until soon it was about the size of a large dog.

"I think it must be some sort of monster from outer space," said Dad one night as he watched the creature swallow its tenth banana. "It seems to be growing in front of my eyes. Suppose it's a Martian sent down to invade the earth!"

Mum laughed. "Does it look as though it could invade the earth all by itself?"

The creature opened its green eyes wide and sneezed loudly.

"It's saying no," said Mussarat crossly. "Really, Dad, you are silly. It might be a monster, but it's a friendly one."

Dad gave a mysterious smile. "But suppose there are more of them in the sweet shop, waiting to hatch out?"

Asif shivered and moved nearer to Shazia. Mum shivered and hugged the baby tight. Dad shivered – and then he began to laugh. And everyone else laughed too. They laughed and laughed until they cried.

Dad wiped his eyes.

"Well, Mussarat," he said, "if it's going to be part of the family you'd better give it a name."

Mussarat smiled. "I already have. I'm going to call him Mr Monster – if he likes it, that is."

The monster's green eyes grew round as

saucers. He gazed at Mussarat and Mussarat gazed back. Then he wrinkled up his yellow nose, sneezed loudly and went to sleep.

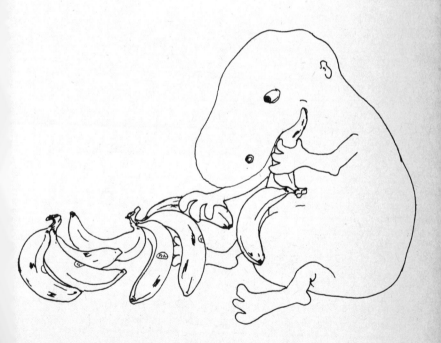

2
Monsters and Magic

Every morning, when Mussarat was getting ready for school, Mr Monster followed her around. He sniffed in her school bag, sniffed at her shoes and sniffed at the bottom of her

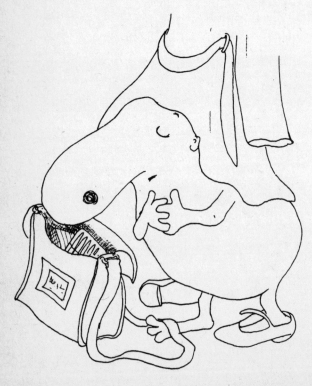

warm green coat hanging on a peg behind the door.

"Why is he doing that?" asked Asif one morning as he was eating his cornflakes.

"To make sure she isn't taking any of his bananas for dinner," said Dad, getting up from the table.

Mr Monster sneezed loudly and looked around, his green eyes twinkling.

"Of course that's not the reason, Dad," said Mussarat, laughing. "He's doing it because he misses me when I'm at school."

Mr Monster shuffled closer to Mussarat and

she stroked him gently. "I wonder what Miss Tackle would say if we took him with us."

"She'd probably faint," said Dad, smiling at the thought.

"Not Miss Tackle," laughed Shazia. She picked up her plimsolls and stuffed them into her bag. "Hurry up, you two, or I'll be late. I want to practise shooting for the netball match this afternoon."

"Couldn't we take him, Mum, just for today?" pleaded Mussarat.

Mum picked up the baby and put him down on the floor.

"I don't really think it's a good idea, Mussarat," she said. "What would he do all day? Besides, I don't think he can even write his name."

The baby crawled towards Mr Monster. "Mmmm," he said.

Mr Monster started to sneeze. He sneezed and sneezed and sneezed and wouldn't stop until at last Mum agreed to write Miss Tackle a letter.

Mussarat opened the door.

"Come on, Mr Monster," she called, and the four set off for school together.

Shazia knocked softly on the headteacher's door. "Come in," boomed a deep voice, and they all went in. Miss Tackle was perched at a large desk in the middle of the room. She peered at the children over the rims of her glasses and beckoned them to come closer.

"Ah, Shazia, and Mussarat, and Asif, and . . ." she dropped her pen and it clattered to the floor.

"Mr Monster," said Mussarat.

Shazia put the letter on Miss Tackle's desk. Miss Tackle opened it and read it quickly.

"No, I can't allow pets in school," she said at last, zipping her lips together firmly.

Sadly the children turned to go, but Mr Monster shuffled forward. He gazed at Miss Tackle, green eyes twinkling, and gave an enormous sneeze.

"Good grief!" she cried, falling back in her chair. Then, as the children watched, she sat up slowly, a strange look clouding her eyes.

"Yessss," she murmured. "Of course, we don't usually allow pets in school, but as it's only for today."

Mussarat smiled.

"Thank you, Miss Tackle," she said, and followed the others to the door as quickly as she could.

In the cloakroom Mussarat's friend Ying Vi was hanging up her coat.

"Hello, Ying Vi," said Mussarat. "This is Mr Monster. He's staying at school with me today."

"Hello, Mr Monster," said Ying Vi. "Come and meet our teacher, Mrs Khan."

Mrs Khan was sitting in the book corner with the register on her knee, waiting for all the children to arrive.

"Good morning, Mrs Khan," said Mussarat.

"Good morning, Mussarat, good morning, Mr Monster. Now sit down quickly everyone."

Everyone sat down, except for a small boy called Robert who was hopping about from leg to leg at the back of the class.

"How do you know his name, Mrs Khan?" he shouted rudely.

Mrs Khan smiled and pressed one finger gently to her lips. After the register she beckoned the children nearer and spoke to them in her soft warm voice. "We have a special visitor in our class today. I hope you'll all be kind to him. His name is Mr Monster and he lives with Mussarat."

"Mr Monster," Robert shouted scornfully. "He doesn't look like a monster to me. Monsters have sharp teeth and fierce faces and the ground shakes like an earthquake when they walk."

Mr Monster scowled. Then he opened his bright green eyes as wide as saucers. His fat yellow body seemed to grow and grow until it threw a gigantic shadow right across the room. Robert stared at the monster and the monster stared back.

"Tell him I'm sorry, Mussarat," Robert whispered. "He's most definitely the fiercest monster I've ever seen."

Then Mrs Khan laughed and the children laughed and Mr Monster sneezed the loudest sneeze Mussarat had ever heard.

"Come on, everybody," said Mrs Khan at last, "it's time to get on with our work."

Some children went to do their number work and some children went to do their writing.

"Can we paint a picture of Mr Monster?" asked Cathy and Yasmin, putting on their aprons.

"I'm sure he won't mind if you do," said Mrs Khan.

Soon everyone wanted to paint his picture, and there were Mr Monsters all over the classroom.

Mussarat and Ying Vi went to do their writing.

"I'm going to write a story about Mr Monster," said Mussarat, writing her name in Urdu at the top of the page.

Ying Vi wrote her name in Chinese. "I'm going to write a story about a monster too, but not a kind monster like yours. A scary one with sharp teeth and long claws who likes to eat little children for his dinner."

Mussarat laughed.

"My monster only likes to eat bananas," she said.

Mr Monster shuffled round the classroom. He watched the children painting, played in the house and listened to Mrs Khan as she helped the red group plant their sunflower seeds.

After a while Mussarat looked up from her writing. Where was Mr Monster? She was just going to call him when suddenly there was a loud crash.

"Aaah!" wailed a voice from under the painting table.

"What's the matter, Fareed?" asked Robert, smirking from behind the sand tray.

"Look at my trousers," cried Fareed, getting up. He was covered in paint. Robert started to laugh. "Shut up," said Fareed, "it's not funny. I must've slipped on something."

Mrs Khan hurried over.

"Don't be unkind, Robert," she scolded. "Now come here, Fareed, and let me wipe it off."

Ying Vi frowned. "I bet it was Robert's fault. Poor Fareed. His mum will go mad when she sees his trousers."

Mr Monster nodded and Mussarat nodded too.

"Oh look," she said, "here comes Mr Walker with our milk."

Mr Walker carried a crate of shiny topped milk bottles down the corridor and into the classroom. All the children looked up. They liked the caretaker and they liked drinking their milk.

"Hello everybody," he called.

"Hello Mr W . . ." they started to reply, then everyone stopped in amazement.

Mr Walker was wobbling backwards and forwards, trying to hold on to the crate.

"Whoaaaa!" he shouted. "Look out, look out!"

"Marbles," cried Mussarat, pointing to the floor. "Robert must've rolled them at Fareed."

The whole class watched horrified as Mr Walker lurched from side to side, trying not to drop the crate of clinking milk bottles. His face turned red, he gave a cry – then, suddenly, Mr Monster sneezed. Six shiny marbles shot across the floor to Mrs Khan's chair and Mr Walker wobbled to a stop.

"Phew, that was a close shave," he said, putting the crate down firmly on a table. He wiped his face with a handkerchief and grinned broadly. "Could've had a nasty accident then, Mrs Khan. Who's the little joker with the marbles?"

Robert crept out from behind the sand tray and began to cry.

"I didn't mean to cause an accident," he sobbed. "I just wanted to play a trick on

Fareed."

"Well, it was a very silly thing to do," said Mrs Khan quietly. "Now come and say you're sorry – to Mr Walker and to Fareed."

At dinner time all the children ate together in the hall. Mr Monster sat with Mussarat and Asif, Ying Vi and her brother Phu Binh.

Mussarat opened her lunch box.

"What have you got today?" asked Ying Vi, opening hers.

Mussarat looked inside. "Two samosas for me and two for Asif, and a biscuit and an apple each." She took out a samosa and gave it to Asif. It was golden brown and crunchy, with soft spicy vegetables inside.

"We've got egg sandwiches today," said Phu Binh and he munched one slowly, enjoying every bite. "What's your Mr Monster got to eat?"

Mussarat smiled. "This is his packed lunch." She delved into her carrier bag and brought out a huge bunch of bananas. "Watch," she said.

Mr Monster's green eyes twinkled and he opened his hungry mouth wide. He took a banana and swallowed it in one gulp, skin

and all. Then another and another until
Mussarat's bag was empty. And when he'd
finished all the children gave a noisy cheer.

At home time it was Shazia's netball
match. Mussarat, Asif and Mr Monster
stayed on to watch.

"It's the semi-final," Miss Tackle told all
the mums and dads. "Westfield School have
a very good team, but I'm sure we're going
to win."

Everybody cheered when the teams came
out. Shazia's team wore blue bands and the
other team wore red. They all stood still until
a teacher blew the whistle, and then the
match began.

"Come on, Shazia," shouted Mussarat.

"Come on, Shazia," shouted Asif.

Mr Monster swayed from side to side, his green eyes shining.

Now the girls ran up and down, twisting and turning, dipping and dodging, stretching and skipping until the red team's captain scored a goal. Shazia scored next, then the red team scored, then Shazia scored again and it was time for them all to have a rest.

"Is our team winning, Mussarat?" asked Asif as they waited for the second half to start.

Mussarat shook her head. "Can't you even count, Asif Hussein!"

Soon the teams came running down the yard and, when the whistle blew, the match began again.

"Come on, Shazia," shouted Mussarat.

"Come on, Shazia," shouted Asif.

And Shazia jumped up high and scored a goal.

"Well done," Miss Tackle boomed, but then the Westfield Captain scored as well.

"Oh no," wailed Mussarat. "It's nearly time for the whistle to blow and no one will have won."

Shazia caught the ball. She ran towards the goal and aimed again.

Mussarat put her hands across her face.

"It missed. I can't look, Asif," she moaned, peeping through her fingers.

For the second time Shazia ran and jumped but, as the ball sailed through the air, the whistle blew.

"Oh no!" cried Asif. "It's going to miss."

Suddenly, Mr Monster sneezed. Like a great brown bird the ball stayed hovering in the sky – and then it soared down gently through the net.

"Good old, Shazia!" Asif shouted. "We've won!"

Mussarat just clapped her hands and smiled.

"And good old Mr Monster too," she said.

3
Mr Monster Goes Shopping

One sunny Saturday morning Mussarat and Mr Monster were playing in the yard.

"Catch," shouted Mussarat as she threw a fat blue ball up high in the air. Mr Monster caught the ball on top of his head. He spun it round and round and round, then tossed it back to Mussarat across the yard.

"They should sign him up for England," said Mr Hussein, watching from the back door.

Mussarat laughed. "He can't play football, Dad, he just likes doing tricks."

Dad looked over his shoulder and scratched his head thoughtfully. The baby was crawling across the kitchen floor towards him, his face covered in sticky red jam.

"Does he know any tricks for sending a baby to sleep?" he asked.

Mussarat laughed again. "What time is

Mum coming back? I promised her I'd go to the shops with Asif."

Dad's face brightened.

"I know," he said, "I'll go to the shops and you and Mr Monster can look after the baby."

"No thank you, Dad. Where's Asif? Asif! Asif!" Mussarat shouted. "It's time to go. NOW!"

The Medina Supermarket stood at the top of the next street. Mum called it her 'Aladdin's Cave' for inside was everything from pans to potatoes, fruit to flour, sugar to samosas. Mussarat swung the door open and they all stepped inside.

"Good morning, Mussarat," called Mr Sharif, the shopkeeper, as he bobbed up and down filling shelves. "All on your own today?"

"No," said Mussarat, taking a basket. "Asif's come with me, he's over there."

Mr Sharif straightened up and stretched his arms in the air with a sigh.

"And where's Shaz . . ." he began, then stopped and stared down the aisle in amazement. "What on earth is that big yellow . . . that big yellow THING doing in MY supermarket?"

"It's not a thing," Mussarat replied indignantly. "It's only Mr Monster."

Mr Sharif chewed furiously at the edges of his wire brush moustache.

"I don't care who it is," he said, wagging a

shaking finger, "I'm not having it in MY supermarket, and that's final!"

"Oh, Mr Sharif," Mussarat pleaded, "he won't . . ." but her words were lost in a sound that roared round the supermarket like a raging lion. Mr Monster had sneezed.

With eyes as big as footballs, Mr Sharif gazed blankly at the door.

"Of . . . course . . . he . . . can . . . stay," he muttered jerkily, then staggered off, robot-fashion, down the aisle.

"What's the matter with Mr Sharif?" asked Asif.

"Nothing much. Just a sore throat, I think. Now what's on Mum's shopping list today?"

"We want a mango."

Mussarat took a mango and sniffed it carefully. Mr Monster sniffed it too.

"And an aubergine."

Mussarat took an aubergine and sniffed it carefully. Mr Monster sniffed it too.

"And some chillies, and some ginger and some okra . . ."

"Hold on," cried Mussarat. "I'll never remember all that." She picked up some chillies and sniffed them carefully.

"Goodness, Mussarat," laughed a voice

from behind her, "you don't have to smell everything, you know!"

"Hello, Mrs Pyke, hello, Davinia," said Asif, pulling a face at Mrs Pyke's baby who was jumping up and down in the trolley. Davinia smiled and jumped up and down even harder.

"Will you go and give the twins 10p each for me, Asif?" asked Mrs Pyke. She pointed to the sweet tray where Leroy and Shantelle were worrying about which sweets were the best to buy.

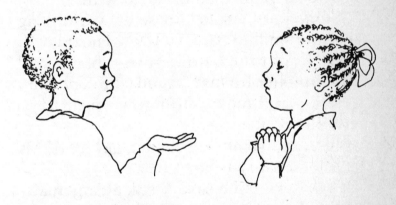

Davinia stopped jumping up and down. She stared at Mr Monster and Mr Monster stared back.

"M. . .m. . m. . .m," she cried, stretching

her arms towards him. Mr Monster shuffled closer to Mussarat and Mrs Pyke began to laugh.

"That's a funny looking animal you've got there, Mussarat, but my Davinia seems to like him." She picked up a bag of shiny red apples and put them into her trolley. Davinia stretched out her arms and picked up a shiny red pepper to go with them.

"Does he like babies?" Mrs Pyke asked, choosing a fat yellow grapefruit to put in her trolley. Davinia stretched out her arms and chose a fat yellow lemon to go with it.

"Sometimes," said Mussarat, wondering what the smiling baby would do next.

Mrs Pyke took a firm green cabbage and put it into her trolley. Davinia stretched out her arms and took a firm green pear to go with it.

Mussarat scratched her head and Mr Monster scratched his.

"Mrs Pyke," she said, "look at Davinia."

Mrs Pyke looked at Davinia. The baby smiled sweetly and Mrs Pyke patted her head.

Mussarat tried again. "Mrs Pyke, look at Davinia, she's . . ."

Mrs Pyke looked at Davinia. The baby smiled sweetly and Mrs Pyke patted her head with one hand and reached out with the other for a tin of beans perched at the top

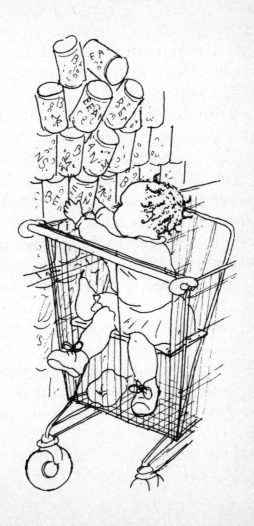

of a wobbly blue pile. Davinia reached out for a tin of beans too and the wobbly blue pile began to wobble.

"Look out, look out!" cried Mussarat as the wobbly blue pile began to sway from side to side.

"What's the matter?" asked Mrs Pyke. She put the tin of beans into her trolley and smiled at Davinia.

"Look out, look out!" cried Mussarat.

Davinia clapped her hands as the wobbly blue pile came flying through the air. Suddenly, Mr Monster sneezed. Davinia stopped clapping and stared at Mr Monster. Now the tins hovered for a moment in the air. Then they began to fly backwards, as if something invisible had caught them in its hands and decided to throw them back.

"M . . m . . m . . m.!" shouted the baby, pointing a chubby finger at the wobbly blue pile.

"What's the matter with you two?" Mrs Pyke sounded puzzled. She turned to look behind her, but the wobbly blue pile had stopped wobbling.

"Nothing, Mrs Pyke," said Mussarat.

Mrs Pyke pushed Davinia to the

checkout and began to unload her shopping.

"Hello, Mrs Pyke, hello, Davinia," said Mr Mr Sharif, sitting down in front of the till.

Mrs Pyke dipped into her trolley. She pulled out a bag of apples and a shiny red pepper, a firm green cabbage and a firm green pear, a fat yellow grapefruit and a fat yellow lemon, a tin of beans, a loaf of bread, a box of cornflakes, a box of eggs and a squashy packet of crunchy biscuits.

Mr Sharif began to add them up. "A bag of apples, a red pepper, a cabbage, a pear . . ."

"Stop, Mr Sharif, stop!" cried Mrs Pyke, gazing at her shopping in amazement. "How on earth did all these things get into my trolley?" Davinia smiled sweetly and swung her legs up and down. "You naughty girl," said Mrs Pyke, "now Leroy and Shantelle will have to put them all back." She shook her finger at the baby and the baby shook her finger too. Then Mr Sharif laughed and Mrs Pyke laughed and Davinia clapped her chubby hands with glee.

Mrs Pyke packed her shopping into a box and put it into the trolley. She pushed the trolley to the door and stopped to wait for Leroy and Shantelle. Mussarat packed her shopping into a shopping bag and waited at the door for Asif.

"Hurry up," shouted Mrs Pyke as the three friends walked towards them. "It's nearly dinner time and I promised your dad I'd get fish and chips today."

"Can I push your trolley to the car for you, Mrs Pyke?" asked Mr Sharif, swinging round in his seat. He smiled at Davinia, and Davinia smiled back. Mr Sharif began to push the trolley through the door and Davinia began jumping up and down.

"Stop that, Davinia," ordered Mrs Pyke. She opened the boot of the car and made a space for the box. Mr Sharif pushed the trolley towards her and Davinia stopped jumping up and down. "Leroy, Shantelle, come and hold the trolley while Mr Sharif lifts the shopping out."

Mr Sharif bent over the side and took the box in his arms. It was heavy, his face turned red and his moustache twitched as he lifted it up.

Shantelle and Leroy got hold of the trolley.

"Let go!" shouted Leroy, giving Shantelle a push. "I want to hold it by myself."

Shantelle pushed him back.

"No, you let go!" she yelled.

They pushed and pulled and pushed until all of a sudden, Mr Sharif let out an enormous yell.

"Wooh!" he shouted, and dropped the box back into the trolley with a loud clang. Then, waving his arms around him like a willow tree on a windy day, Mr Sharif toppled to the ground. Shantelle and Leroy were so startled that they let go of the trolley.

"Go, go, go," shouted Davinia, jumping up and down. And the trolley went hurtling down the street.

Mrs Pyke watched it open-mouthed.

"Davinia," she called faintly. "Davinia."

"My trolley," groaned Mr Sharif, rubbing his head with one hand and holding his back with the other.

"The shopping!" all the children cried together, as they watched the trolley bouncing up and down.

Davinia gripped the handle like a racing driver at the Monte Carlo rally.

"Go, go, go," she shouted, and the trolley did, faster and faster, nearer and nearer to the busy road that lay at the bottom of the street.

Mussarat stared at Mr Monster and Mr Monster stared back. And then, with a sound that shook the air like thunder on a Summer's day, Mr Monster sneezed.

Suddenly the runaway trolley came hurtling to a stop.

"Go, go, go," shouted Davinia, but the trolley refused to budge.

"It's stopped. Thank goodness!" cried Mrs Pyke, running down the street as fast as she could. Leroy and Shantelle followed, with Mr Sharif limping close behind.

"Oh, Davinia, you're safe," said Mrs Pyke as she pulled the struggling baby out of the trolley.

"Go, go, go," shouted Davinia, jumping up and down in her arms.

Mrs Pyke held Davinia tight.

"Now stop that," she ordered, and carried the baby back to the top of the street. Leroy and Shantelle followed, pushing the trolley with Mr Sharif close behind.

Mrs Pyke packed her shopping away and shut the boot of the car with a loud bang.

"Now, children, in you get," she said, "or it will be too late to get those fish and chips."

The twins leaped into the car and waved goodbye to Mussarat and Asif. And Davinia waved goodbye to Mr Monster.

"M . . m . . m," she shouted, jumping up and down in her seat.

"You must bring Mr Monster round to play with Davinia, Mussarat," said Mrs Pyke as she climbed into the front. "They really seem to get on well together."

42

Mr Monster shuffled closer to Mussarat and Mussarat began to laugh.

"What's the matter with you?" asked Asif.

"Nothing," said Mussarat, putting her arm around Mr Monster. "It's really nothing at all!"

4
Welcome to the Family

Mussarat opened her eyes. It was dark in the bedroom, but her big sister Shazia was already up and dressed.

"Come on, lazybones," she said. "It takes a long time to get there, and Dad wants to set off as early as he can."

Mussarat threw back her covers and jumped out of bed. This was the day she'd been waiting for ever since the summer holidays had begun. They were going to stay with Grandma and Grandad in their big house in London, and her aunties and uncles and all her cousins would be there as well.

"Are you putting your new salwar kameez on today?" asked Shazia, as she opened the bedroom door.

Mussarat nodded. Her new salwar kameez lay over a chair at the side of the bed. The dress was pink, and covered in small golden flowers that shone in the dark. The trousers were pink too, and gathered at the ankles with a broad band of gold.

Mussarat put them on and looked at herself in the mirror. She was so excited she twirled round and round. One day, her dad had promised, they would go and visit her other grandma and grandad who lived in Pakistan. But today they were going to London and Mussarat could hardly wait!

"I wonder what Grandma will do when she sees Mr Monster," said Asif as he climbed into the back of the van.

Dad wrinkled his forehead in a deep frown. "I think she'll probably scream."

"Oh dear," said Mum, strapping the struggling baby into his seat, "then perhaps we ought to leave him behind."

"What do you say, Mussarat?" Dad's brown eyes twinkled.

"Honestly, Dad, you are a tease," said Mussarat crossly. "I think she'll like him just as much as we do."

The van roared off down the road and soon they were on the motorway. Mussarat looked out of the window. Cars flashed past, and gigantic lorries raced after them, their great wheels chugging round and round as they tried their best to catch up.

"Are we nearly there yet?" asked Asif, shuffling in his seat.

"Of course not, silly," said Shazia. "We've

only just started."

"Why don't you play some games," suggested Mum, "or sing some of the songs you learn at school?"

Mussarat smiled. "I spy with my little eye," she began, and soon everyone wanted to play.

After a while Shazia started to sing, and the baby clapped his hands with glee. Asif and Mussarat joined in and Mr Monster swayed from side to side. The singing van sped down the motorway, humming and whistling on its way to London. Dad wanted to sing too, but the children wouldn't let him.

"You sound like a tiger with a toothache," laughed Shazia. "Just go la, la, la instead,"

"La, la, la," sang Dad, "la, la, laaaaaa . . . oh no!"

Suddenly the van began to lurch up and down. It coughed and spluttered, sneezed and wheezed until Dad steered it into one of the motorway service stops.

"Everybody out," he called, "but watch out for cars coming in."

Dad lifted up the bonnet and started to fiddle with the engine. The three children sat on the grass near their van and counted the cars as they came in. Mum walked up and down with the baby and Mr Monster shuffled round and round.

"Right," said Dad at last, "that should do it." And he climbed back into the van. Whirr, moaned the engine, whirr, whirr, whirr.

Dad scratched his head and frowned. "I can't understand it, I really can't."

He began to fiddle with the engine again. Whirr, moaned the engine, whirr, whirr, whirr.

"Can't you get it to go, dear?" said Mum kindly, peering under the bonnet. The baby peered too.

Dad scratched his head and sighed. "No, I'll have to call the breakdown service out."

Mum peered a little further under the bonnet and the baby peered too. "Is it something to do with all these wires here?"

"Don't touch!" yelled Dad, leaping out of the van as if his trousers were on fire.

Suddenly, Mr Monster sneezed. Mussarat turned to look at him and winked.

"Try to start the van again, Dad," she said. "You never know, Mum might've made it work!"

"Huh!" snorted Dad, and climbed back into his seat.

Brrr, sang the engine, brrr, brrr, brrr.

"Hooray!" shouted Shazia. "Mum's a mechanic, she's got it to start."

"Huh!" snorted Dad, and drove off with a

scowl down the motorway again.

At six o'clock the van drew up outside a tall terraced house whose broad steps rose steeply to a bright blue door.

"We're here!" Shazia shouted excitedly. Just at that moment the bright blue door opened and a smiling Grandma and Grandad came down to greet them.

"Come in, everybody," said Grandma and led the way down a narrow hall to a large room full of aunties and uncles and cousins and the longest table Mussarat had ever seen.

While Mum put the baby to bed Grandma and all the aunties brought dish after dish of delicious smelling food until Mussarat was sure that the table would begin to complain.

"And last but not least," laughed Grandma, putting a large glass bowl in the middle of it all, "some bananas for my new friend, Mr Monster."

Mr Monster's green eyes twinkled and he gave a little bow before opening his hungry mouth wide. He popped the bananas in one by one and soon the large glass bowl was empty.

"Ugh!" cried Mussarat's cousin, Razina,

50

moving away as fast as she could. "It even eats banana skin as well."

Mussarat scowled. "His name is Mr Monster and he always eats everything he's given."

"Well, I don't want it sitting next to me."

Razina sat down at the bottom of the table and waited for the meal to begin.

Soon everyone started to eat and talk and laugh and joke and a hum of happiness ran round the room.

"Eat your vegetables, Razina, dear," said Aunty Azra as she helped herself to one of Grandma's round fat buttery chapattis.

"I don't want to eat my vegetables," moaned Razina, pushing them to the side of her plate.

Aunty Azra helped herself to another of Grandma's round fat buttery chapattis. "Eat your rice then, Razina, please."

"I don't want to eat my rice," moaned Razina, pushing it to the side of her plate.

Aunty Azra helped herself to another of Grandma's round fat buttery chapattis and gave it to Razina. "Eat one of Grandma's special chapattis then, Razina. I know you'll like it."

"I don't want to eat one of Grandma's special chapattis," moaned Razina and pushed her plate away.

Aunty Azra smiled at Grandma. "I don't know what's the matter with Razina today," she said brightly. "She usually eats everything she's given."

Mussarat winked at Mr Monster and Mr Monster winked back. Then he wrinkled up his yellow nose and sneezed.

Suddenly Razina sat up as straight as a soldier on parade. She pulled her plate towards her and gobbled up everything in sight.

"Can I have some more, please," she said, staring at Aunty Azra as if she was in a trance.

Aunty Azra smiled at Grandma and piled Razina's plate as high as she could. Without so much as a nod or a blink, Razina munched

her way through miles of savoury rice and mountains of spicy vegetables, a mound of juicy chicken and three of Grandma's round fat buttery chapattis.

Aunty Azra smiled at Grandma. "Razina's such a good girl, she always eats everything she's given."

Mr Monster winked at Mussarat and Mussarat winked back. Then his green eyes twinkled and Mussarat began to laugh.

"What's so funny?" asked Asif as he helped himself to the last chapatti.

"Nothing," said Mussarat wiping her eyes. "It's really nothing at all."

They were staying at Grandma's for a whole week, but the time passed too quickly for Mussarat. One day Dad took them to Buckingham Palace and Asif was sure he'd seen the Queen.

But the days Mussarat liked best of all were when Grandma told them stories about when she was a little girl in Pakistan. Mussarat thought it must have been lovely to live in a small village where everyone was friendly, and to sleep outside under the stars when it was warm.

One night, after Grandma had tucked them up in bed and all the house was quiet, Mussarat dreamed that *she* was in Pakistan, on a flat roof beneath the stars with a big yellow moon so near she could almost touch it. And as she stared at the sky the moon came nearer and nearer and nearer until Mussarat was so hot she couldn't breathe.

All of a sudden she woke up with a start. Why did she feel so thirsty, she wondered, and climbed out of bed to get a drink. It was dark on the stairs and Mussarat tiptoed down as quiet as a mouse. The whole house lay sleeping. Even Mr Monster, curled up on his bed behind the kitchen door, had his eyes shut tight as Mussarat crept over to the sink.

It was then that she heard it. A faint creaking sound, as if someone was opening and closing a cupboard door. Then the rustling started. Mussarat's heart began to thump. It seemed to be coming from the room next door.

What should she do? It might only be Grandad who couldn't get to sleep, or Mum with the baby who was cutting some more teeth. Or it might be . . . Mussarat shuddered . . . it might be . . .

Crash! A sound like breaking glass brought Mr Monster to his feet. He lumbered swiftly into the room next door with Mussarat shivering beside him. She stretched out her hand to feel for the switch and suddenly the whole room was flooded with light.

Over by the open window a man stood shading his eyes with his hand. In the other he held a bulging sports bag and on the floor beside him, broken into tiny, shining pieces, lay Grandma's best china teapot.

"Help!" shouted the man, staring at Mr Monster. "The blooming house is haunted."

And in a flash he dropped his bag and dived for the open window.

"Oh no!" cried Mussarat. "He's getting away!"

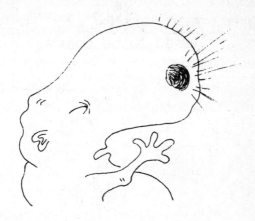

Suddenly, Mr Monster sneezed. As quick as a flash the window swooped down and caught the man across his middle. He kicked and shouted, shouted and kicked, until the whole house came to see who was making that terrible noise. Everybody laughed when they saw him.

"Let me go," he cried, waving his arms and legs around like a capsized tortoise.

Dad dialled 999 and soon two policemen came to take him away.

"You're a very brave little girl," they said to Mussarat, "catching a burglar all by yourself."

"I didn't do it all by myself, Mr Monster helped." Mussarat winked at Mr Monster and Mr Monster winked back.

"Frightened the life out of me, it did," complained the burglar, rubbing his back with his hands. "Things like that should be kept in a zoo."

"It's a good job for us he isn't," laughed Grandma and everybody else laughed too.

Next day Mum and Dad bought Grandma a new china teapot to say thank you for a lovely holiday. And Grandma gave Mussarat a tiny wooden elephant that came all the way from Pakistan.

"And this is for Mr Monster," she said, holding out the biggest bunch of bananas they'd ever seen. "Welcome to the family!"

"Welcome to the family!" said everyone.

Mr Monster looked at them and smiled, his green eyes twinkling, and gave them all a little bow.